# The House without a Christmas Tree

OTHER YEARLING BOOKS YOU WILL ENJOY:

GIVE US A GREAT BIG SMILE, ROSY COLE,
  *Sheila Greenwald*
WILL THE REAL GERTRUDE HOLLINGS PLEASE STAND UP?,
  *Sheila Greenwald*
ANASTASIA AGAIN!, *Lois Lowry*
ANASTASIA AT YOUR SERVICE, *Lois Lowry*
ANASTASIA, ASK YOUR ANALYST, *Lois Lowry*
THE ONE HUNDREDTH THING ABOUT CAROLINE,
  *Lois Lowry*
TAKING CARE OF TERRIFIC, *Lois Lowry*
COURAGE, DANA, *Susan Beth Pfeffer*
JUST BETWEEN US, *Susan Beth Pfeffer*
WHAT DO YOU DO WHEN YOUR MOUTH WON'T OPEN?,
  *Susan Beth Pfeffer*

YEARLING BOOKS/YOUNG YEARLINGS/YEARLING CLASSICS are
designed especially to entertain and enlighten young people.
Charles F. Reasoner, Professor Emeritus of Children's Litera-
ture and Reading, New York University, is consultant to
this series.

For a complete listing of all Yearling titles,
write to Dell Readers Service, P.O. Box 1045,
South Holland, Illinois 60473.

# THE HOUSE WITHOUT A CHRISTMAS TREE

## GAIL ROCK
### illustrated by Charles C. Gehm

A YEARLING BOOK

*With acknowledgments to Alan Shayne and Eleanor Perry, who did so much to bring "Addie" to life.*

Published by
Dell Publishing Co., Inc.
1 Dag Hammarskjold Plaza
New York, New York 10017

Yearling ® TM 913705, Dell Publishing Co., Inc.

ISBN: 0-440-43394-0

Reprinted by arrangement with Alfred A. Knopf, Inc.

Printed in the United States of America

November 1985

10 9 8

CW

*For Grandma and Dad*

# The House without a Christmas Tree

# Prologue

I'M AN ARTIST NOW, and I live and work in the city. It's a landscape of cement and noise and crowds, all very different and very far away from the little town where I grew up—Clear River, Nebraska, population: 1500.

Clear River was surrounded by cornfields and cattle and open sky. The tallest building in town was only three stories high. Most of the streets were unpaved, and we didn't even have a traffic light. We didn't need one. Every day the Union Pacific Streamliners roared through, but they never stopped in Clear River.

I often think of that little town, and that special Christmas in 1946, when I was ten years old.

# Chapter One

CARLA MAE AND I were sitting in our little kitchen at the old wooden table, with our spoons poised in mid-air. In front of each of us was a hard-boiled egg perched in an egg cup. We both stared intently at the faces we had drawn on our eggs. The longer the stare, the better the hex.

"Who's yours today?" she asked.

"Billy Wild," I said, making a face. "Who's yours?"

"Mine's Delmer Doakes," she answered, still staring at her egg.

"Ready?" I whispered.

"Ready!" said Carla Mae, and we both smashed our spoons down in unison on the poor eggheads. I crunched Billy a good one, but at the last second Carla Mae hesitated, and only gave Delmer's pointy head a firm tap.

"You chickened out!" I said. "You're supposed to smack him!"

Carla Mae blushed. "Well, I just like to do it all over in little bitty cracks, like he has wrinkles," and she daintily tapped all around the sides of her egg until Delmer looked 107 years old.

"Oh, you just don't want to smash Delmer because you like

him," I said disgustedly, and gave my egg another smash, knocking the top right off.

"Yeah, well, you like Billy Wild too," Carla Mae said in her ickiest voice. "You're always looking at him in class."

"I am not! I just look at him to stick out my tongue. I think he's a rotten creep!"

"Adelaide!" said my Grandmother from across the kitchen. "Such talk!"

Carla Mae and I giggled, and dug into our eggs. Carla Mae was ten years old too, and my best friend in the fifth grade. Her family had moved in next door to us two years ago, in 1944, and now we were inseparable. We always walked to and from school together, and often ate lunch with each other.

Carla Mae's family had opened up a whole new world to me. I was an only child, but she had five younger brothers and sisters and another on the way. I learned about diapers and bottles, and that mothers shouldn't climb ladders when they are pregnant, and about eating horrible things for lunch like ketchup and mayonnaise sandwiches on white bread, and how to fight off five other people if you wanted to play with the electric train set, and that if you had a big family, someone always walked in on you when you were in the bathroom and that it didn't matter.

I loved the uproar, and I always felt lonely when I went home to our quiet house. Carla Mae already liked boys, and I pretended to share her enthusiasm, though I really thought it was kind of dumb. She taught me to swear, and I helped her with arithmetic.

She liked coming to my house because it was the opposite of hers. It was small, only a four-room bungalow, and almost

threadbare, but it was quiet and orderly, and my grandmother always fixed a hot lunch for us. She was especially fond of feeding us eggs, which she thought were good for what ailed you, and which we didn't much like. The face-drawing was intended to make egg-eating more interesting, and like a lot of Grandma's eccentric ideas, it worked very well.

When we were at Carla Mae's house we made our own lunch from whatever we could find in the refrigerator. We would fix Dagwood sandwiches dripping with sardines and peanut butter and cheese and brown sugar and pickled shrimp and every other thing we could find—horrible, delicious combinations. Her mother was too busy changing diapers and warming bottles to notice.

But this particular December day we were having lunch at my house because we needed to have a serious discussion about Christmas shopping. It was only a week before Christmas, and Friday would be our last day of school before vacation. That was the big day when we exchanged presents in our class, and we each had to buy a present for the person whose name we had drawn.

The names were to be kept secret, but Carla Mae and I always told each other everything, so I knew she had drawn Jerry Walsh, and she knew I had drawn Tanya Smithers. Jerry was an OK boy, so she was going to buy him a green plastic pencil box we had seen at the dimestore, but I was stumped about Tanya.

"We have to get them today," said Carla Mae, "so we'll have time to wrap them tonight."

"I can't think of anything horrible enough for Tanya

Smithers," I said. We couldn't stand Tanya. She was very snobbish and was always taking dancing lessons and showing off. "Addie," said Grandma. "I want you to buy her something nice now, no funny business." She came over from the stove and poured bowls of alphabet soup for us.

All conversation stopped while we frantically stirred through our soup to see who could fish out the letters of her name first. It was bad luck if you couldn't find all the letters of your own name in the first bowl.

"I'm first!" shouted Carla Mae, and I looked over at her plate, where she had spelled out C-A-R-L-A in wet alphabet noodles.

"That's only half your name!" I said, and hurried to finish my A-D-D-I-E. I hated my nickname worse than my whole name, Adelaide, but it was a lot easier to spell in a hurry.

"You can't use your nickname!" said Carla Mae.

"I can if you can use half your name!"

"Mae is my middle name," she said, looking very smug.

"You're both right," Grandma interrupted. "Now finish up or you're going to be late getting back to school."

"I think I'll get Tanya some gloves," I said to Carla Mae.

"Ick. Who wants gloves?"

"That's why I'm getting them, dodo. Really dumb ones. Like dark brown wool—old lady gloves with no designs on them."

"Yack . . ." said Carla Mae, grabbing her throat as if she were going to be ill. We both giggled. Tanya would hate dark brown gloves.

"Addie," said Grandma, disapprovingly. "I don't know what gets into you!"

"Well," I said. "You can't get anything neat for a fifty cent limit. Besides, Tanya is my worst friend in the fifth grade."

Grandma shook her head and sank down in her chair.

"Oh, yo," she sighed. She often said that, and we never did know what it meant. It seemed to be an all-purpose phrase that even she couldn't quite explain.

Grandma was in her seventies, short and shapeless and always slightly disheveled, but full of vigor. She had lived with my father and me since my mother died shortly after I was born. Grandma always wore a strange conglomeration of clothes that were either homemade or handed down from my aunts. She was always running up things on her treadle sewing machine, and some of her clothes were pieced together from remnants—eye-popping combinations of color and design. She was particularly expert at whittling down the worn edges of a garment and making it into something smaller. When one of her flowered cotton housedresses began to wear out, she would hack out the collar and sleeves, and it would suddenly be a slip. When that started to go, it became a bib apron and then a smaller apron, and then a dust cap for her hair and then a quilted pot holder (which she called a "hot pad") and in its final incarnation, the tiny remaining scrap would go into a patchwork quilt or a braided rag rug. Any piece of fabric that found its way into our house wouldn't get out again for a good fifty years if Grandma got her hands on it.

To complete her costume of housedress, apron and dust cap, she always wore hand-me-down nylons with runs in them, usually with Indian moccasins. She was only five-feet-two and weighed only a shade over 100 pounds, but she stomped when she walked, and the moccasins enhanced her pile-driver style. The whole house shook when she pounded around in a hurry. She felt that she was too old to bother about how she looked around the house, and that it was wasteful for her to wear good clothes. I was sometimes embarrassed to have other people see the way she dressed, but Carla Mae was used to her by now.

Carla Mae was sliding other letters around on her plate, trying to see if she could spell out the rest of her name.

"What are you getting for Christmas?" she asked me.

"I want a microscope set and some cowboy boots," I said loudly, looking quickly to see if Grandma had heard, "but I always get a dumb blouse or something."

"Cowboy boots!" screamed Carla Mae triumphantly. "You just want cowboy boots because Billy Wild has them. I knew it! You like him!"

Grandma looked up at us, trying to hide a smile, and I blushed furiously.

"I do not!" I shouted back. "I like the kind of boots Roy Rogers and Dale Evans wear. That's where I saw them!"

Before that discussion could go any further, I gulped down the rest of my soup and lunged out of my chair.

"Come on, we'll be late!" I said to Carla Mae, and we headed for the living room to struggle back into our heavy coats and boots.

"How come you haven't got your Christmas tree up yet?" Carla Mae asked.

"Oh," I said, trying not to show embarrassment. "We don't want one."

"How come?" she asked, sounding surprised.

"They're just a waste of money," I said, parroting the argument my father had given me. "Besides, we're going to Uncle Will's to open presents, and he has a tree." I could tell the reasoning wasn't going over any better with Carla Mae than it had with me. We didn't have a tree the Christmas before either, but we had been in Des Moines visiting my aunt, so I didn't have to answer any questions then.

"My dad wouldn't dream of not having a tree," she said. "Mom says he acts just like a little boy at Christmas time."

"Well," I said huffily, "My dad's grown up and he acts grown up."

"Where are you going to put your presents?" she asked.

"Oh, we pile them all up on the writing desk," I said lamely.

"I bet you're the only person in town without a tree," said Carla Mae.

"Jesus didn't have a Christmas tree," I replied.

"He didn't?" she said, surprised.

"Of course not, dodo!"

"Would your Dad buy you a tree if you wanted one?" she asked.

"Sure," I said, trying to sound confident.

I was sure Grandma was listening from the kitchen, because she suddenly became very quiet. I didn't want to go on with my explanations to Carla Mae, so I pretended to have problems fastening the buckles on my galoshes.

I knew that asking my father to buy a Christmas tree had become a forbidden subject in our house. Of course that wouldn't stop me from asking him again, because I was always bringing up forbidden subjects, but I just hadn't figured out how to approach it this year. He had never let us have a Christmas tree as far back as I could remember. I would ask every Christmas, and he would say no, and Grandma would look at him as though she were displeased, but she never interfered beyond that. He would say it was a waste of money because we were going to Uncle Will's house, but I knew we were hardly that poor, and that there was something more to it than the cost. I would keep trying, and he would keep getting angry.

That seemed to happen a lot to my father and me. I could never figure out just what the trouble was. As far as I could tell, I talked in plain sentences. I was, after all, the smartest person in the fifth grade, and I was very good in English. But my father seldom understood what I *meant*. And he seemed to have the same trouble getting his ideas across to me. It was as if our words to each other passed through some mysterious spy code machine that made them come out all scrambled at the other end.

Sometimes I would look through the family photograph album and see pictures of him and my mother together in the ten years before I was born. They would be fishing or sitting in an old roadster or having a picnic, and there was even a funny picture of him all dressed up as the bride in a mock wedding. They seemed to have had fun then, but he was not like that when I knew him. I always wondered why he was so different to me than he seemed in those photographs.

As I finished buckling my big, black galoshes, I noticed Grandma standing in the doorway watching. She had that expression that always seemed to be half suspicion, half amusement. That was the way she looked when she knew I was up to something.

"You get something nice for Tanya, now," she said.

I nodded my head, but made a face, and Carla Mae and I raced out the door.

The school was only two blocks away, but it took us a long time to get there. It had snowed in Clear River the night before, and the snowplow had pushed big ridges of snow up along both sides of the streets. We had to climb up on the highest piles and have a shoving contest to see who could stay on top longest. Soon some of the other kids walking back to school came by, and we had a full-scale King of the Mountain game going, with one person trying to stay on top of the pile and shove everyone else down. Only the King on top was allowed to use the snow clods for ammunition, but it was perilous to bend over and pick one up, because you were liable to a sneak attack of pushing from behind.

By the time the school bell rang, we were exhausted and sweating from the exertion, and we ran gasping toward the schoolhouse door, taking in great gulps of lung-searing, cold air. There was a long, narrow, dark cloakroom outside our class-room, and at this time of the day, all twenty-seven of us in the fifth grade seemed to be in there at once, giggling and shoving and struggling out of our snow-caked galoshes and wet wool, smelling like a steaming herd of goats.

If any fights were going to break out during the day, they almost always started here. There was something about that dank, crowded space that brought out the devil in everyone. Someone was always getting punched or kicked or bopped over the head with a book, and I was always getting my pigtails pulled, especially by Billy Wild.

I was standing on one leg like a stork, trying to pull off my left boot without pulling off my shoe and sock too, when Jerry Walsh gave Billy a big shove and pushed him right into me. I went sprawling on the floor, getting the seat of my blue jeans wet in the puddles of melting snow, and Jerry giggled and shouted, "Billy's beating up Addie!"

"You got me all wet, you dodo!" I shouted, and threw my boot at the two of them. Suddenly we heard Miss Thompson's high heels clicking across the varnished floor of the classroom in our direction. She was always on guard for fights in the cloakroom, and I quickly retrieved my boot and we all stood up and looked very busy at neatly hanging our coats on the hooks along the wall. Miss Thompson gave us a little smile that said she knew better, and we all filed quickly into the classroom.

Our class Christmas tree was in the corner by Miss Thompson's desk. It was over seven feet tall and loaded down with all the ornaments that we had been making in art class for the last month. It had colored paper chains; strings of cranberries and popcorn; stars, bells and candles of colored construction paper trimmed with glitter and silver foil we had saved from gum wrappers and our fathers' cigarette packages; lacy white snowflakes cut from folded paper and even a string of lights Miss Thompson had brought from home. Underneath were most of the presents that we would open that Friday.

I thought it was the most beautiful tree I had ever seen and would have been happy with one half that size. I started thinking then about some dramatic approach to use on Dad that night.

# Chapter Two

MISS THOMPSON CALLED US to order as the afternoon bell rang and reminded us that our presents for the class present exchange must be under the tree by Friday morning. I had been elected to the committee to buy Miss Thompson a gift, and we planned to shop for it the next day.

We all adored Miss Thompson, and she adored us right back. At least we thought she did. She was tall and pretty, with dark hair worn in a style just like Betty Grable's, the famous movie star. Of course Betty was blonde, and Miss Thompson was a brunette, but we didn't think the comparison was strained.

All Miss Thompson's suits and dresses had fashionable padded shoulders, and the seams of her stockings were always straight. She wore Evening in Paris cologne and always had nice corsages of artificial flowers on her lapels. Miss Thompson tried not to play favorites with any of us, but I was pretty sure she especially liked me, and I spent a lot of time after school helping clean up and smacking blackboard erasers together out on the fire escape.

"We don't want anyone to be left out of the gift exchange," Miss Thompson was saying, "So remember that Santa Claus will be here Friday."

We all giggled, thinking it very funny to have a Santa Claus at our age. In fact, Santa would be played by Delmer Doakes, who was the chubbiest boy in the class, and Carla Mae's true love.

"Remember," Miss Thompson reminded us, "the maximum you can spend for the person whose name you drew is fifty cents."

"What's the minimum?" asked Delmer, being silly.

"Zero!" said Billy Wild from behind me.

Everybody giggled at his dumb joke, and I turned around and made a face at him.

"You're so parsimonious!" I said. It was a new word we had just learned in vocabulary that morning, and I was delighted to find an opportunity to use it so soon. I was very good in vocabulary, and always tried to use new words right away—especially if I could use them on Billy. He was always showing off his cowboy boots because he was the only kid in class with a horse. I would have given anything for a horse, but even getting a pair of cowboy boots seemed unlikely.

Billy made a face back at me and gave one of my pigtails a yank. It always annoyed him that I usually got better grades than he did. Whenever I got 100 on a test he would call me "teacher's pet," and I would plot to get back at him the rest of the day. I knew I was the best student in the class, but I had been taught at home to be modest about it, so I took the attitude that my smartness was just an annoyance I had to put up with, like being born with freckles or six toes. I couldn't help it if I got good grades all the time, it just happened.

I knew if I didn't get straight A's, I would be in trouble with my father. My mother had been valedictorian of her high school class, and he expected me to live up to that. He hardly ever talked about her to me, but that was one thing he had told me. He had never finished high school himself, and I think he wanted me to make up for that too.

I got home right after school that afternoon, because Grandma had to fit my costume for the church Christmas pageant. I was playing the lead angel, and while I was busy wrapping foil around my coat-hanger halo, she was fitting my white angel costume. She had made it from an old sheet, sewed up on her sewing machine. She sat at the machine in the little bedroom we shared, and I stood on a kitchen chair in front of her so she could make the hem even all around. I turned around and around as we talked.

"You kids will be stopping by here tomorrow night to sing Christmas carols, won't you?" she asked.

"I don't know if we'll be here or not," I said, trying to sound casual.

"Why not?" Grandma asked, sounding surprised.

"Well, I'm ashamed to have them come here."

"My glory! Why? You're not ashamed of your old grandmother, are you?" she asked.

"No! It's just . . . well, I'm ashamed we don't have a Christmas tree. We're probably the only people in town who don't."

"If you don't come here and sing carols, your Dad is going to feel awful bad!" she said.

"It serves him right!" I said angrily. "I feel bad not having a Christmas tree!"

"Addie! Being vengeful is not Christian! What would Reverend Teasdale say if he heard you talk like that? I'll bet you wouldn't be playing the lead angel in the Christmas pageant."

I gave a big sigh and went on fixing my halo. I knew the only reason I got to play the lead angel anyway was because I was the tallest and could hold the star of Bethlehem up higher than anyone else, but Grandma thought it was some kind of honor for good behavior, so I let her go on thinking that. She took churchgoing very seriously, and always insisted that I go to Sunday School and church and young people's Bible-study classes. She didn't go very often herself because she could no longer hear or see well enough to participate in the services, but she read her Bible faithfully every day.

When she was reading, she would push her thick glasses up on top of her head, hold her Bible just a few inches from her face and squint at it, sometimes through a magnifying glass. When she found a verse she particularly liked, she would get a stubby little pencil, which she sharpened with a paring knife, and scrawl the verse on a little scrap of paper. She would add that to all her other little scraps of paper. She was always cutting out recipes and patterns from the newspaper and little tidbits of information, four or five line stories that newspapers refer to as "fillers," which she thought were the best part of the paper. It would be something about Bolivia producing 600,000 tons of coal last year or that the largest tomato in the world was grown by Mr. Jonas Phillips of Rhode Island.

She tried to keep all these scraps of paper in one place, in a cigar box on the floor near the sofa, but somehow they always found their way to other parts of the house. You never knew when you were going to suddenly be confronted with a verse from Isaiah or part of a Psalm or a recipe for chocolate meat loaf or a flash about Mr. Phillips' tomato.

My dad, who was terribly neat and organized, found this quite an irritation, but I rather liked it. I thought it was a pretty good way to get inspired in the middle of dusting under the bed—suddenly finding some message like, "Consider the lilies of the field." In fact, I always wondered if Grandma didn't scatter her scraps around on purpose, as a kind of supplementary education project of her own. It would have been just like her, because she liked being in charge of everything, and when she couldn't do it one way, she would find another.

I took after her in that respect, and between the two of us, I guess we kept my dad on his toes. He often found himself not knowing quite what to expect next, caught between two rambunctious and unpredictable females.

I told Grandma then that I would think about our coming to the house to sing Christmas carols.

"You'd better come," she said.

I didn't say anything for a few moments, as she worked on the hem.

"Why is Dad so parsimonious?" I asked suddenly.

"That's a pretty fancy word."

"We learned it in vocabulary this week. It means stingy."

"He's not stingy," she said. "He's careful. He remembers what it's like to be poor. Folks had a bad time back in the Depression."

"Well, he's not poor now! He has almost $6,000 in the bank!"

"How do you know?" she asked, sounding surprised.

"He was teaching me how to write a check, and he had all his papers out, and I saw the balance in his bankbook."

"You shouldn't be so nosy about other people's business."

"Well, I'd have to be blindfolded not to see it!" I said. "You know, the other kids think it's pretty peculiar."

"What?"

"That we never have a Christmas tree in this house!"

"Just say we're going to Uncle Will's and sharing his tree."

"That sounds so dumb."

"You don't need to give a fig what others think," she said. "Now, let's see how this looks."

I twirled around on the chair. "How do you know angels dressed like this?" I asked.

"Tells in the Bible," Grandma said. "If you paid attention in Sunday School, you'd know too."

"It doesn't say they wore old bed sheets!" I said, twirling around some more.

"Stop fidgeting!" she said.

"I bet angels wore robes of pure silk!"

"Addie, will you stand still!"

"Do you think Dad might do it this year? Might buy me a tree?"

"Oh, yo!" she said, wearily. "I wouldn't nag him about it."

"I don't nag. He never listens to me! I have to ask him everything a million times!" I said. "He doesn't care anything about me. He never pays any attention to me . . ."

Grandma looked at me disapprovingly. "He buys your food

and clothes, don't he? Pays the doctor bills . . . all the bills in this house."

"But he doesn't *talk* to me!" I said, trying to make her understand. "I'm a person too, you know. I like to be talked to."

Grandma went on working on the hem, and I could tell she was hoping I'd give up the idea.

"You said Dad always bought my mother a tree. How come he wasn't stingy with her?"

"It was different then," she said quietly. "They always spent Christmas Day at home. Now we go to Uncle Will's."

"Do you think he might do it this year, though?"

"Well," Grandma sighed. "I s'pose there's no harm in asking."

I hugged her, thankful she was at least part way on my side. "OK! Tonight I'm going to implore him to buy a tree! Implore means beg, but it sounds better."

With that big decision made, I jumped down from the chair and struck a crazy pose in front of the old mirror on our dresser. I didn't think I looked much like an angel.

# Chapter Three

I GOT MORE AND MORE NERVOUS as the afternoon wore on. Dad would soon be home, and I would have to make my move. I was looking anxiously out the living room window, watching for his truck in the driveway, when Billy Wild came along delivering newspapers. He usually made the rounds on his bike, but he couldn't get through the heavy snow that afternoon, so he was pulling his canvas bag of papers along on his sled. He was wearing galoshes over his cowboy boots, and I knew it was killing him to have to cover them up for even a second.

At most of the houses along his route, he would just put the paper between the storm door and the inside door, or put it in a protected place like the milk box, but he usually knocked on the door at our house and handed it to me, and we'd talk a minute or two. I didn't know why we always talked to each other, because if anyone had asked us, we would have said we didn't even like each other. But for some reason, we would yak on about nothing.

Today, though, I wasn't in the mood for any idle chatter. As soon as he knocked on the door, I yanked it open, grabbed the paper out of his hand, said "thanks," and practically slammed the door in his face before he could say a word. He just stood there on the porch giving me a disgusted look. I stuck my tongue out at him, and he did the same back and turned around and went down the steps. I watched him as he grabbed the rope of his sled and went on down the street.

I plopped nervously onto the sofa with the newspaper and tried to concentrate on Dick Tracy, but the approaching confrontation with Dad kept interfering.

When he finally came home, I tried to stay out of his way. I invented things to do, like picking lint off my sweater and polishing my brown oxfords, which I usually did about once a year. I hardly said a word all through dinner. Grandma kept looking over at me to see if I was going to take the plunge, and I would pretend to be interested in my mashed potatoes, which in reality I hated with a passion.

When dinner was over, Dad went into the living room to read the paper, and I got very interested in helping with the dishes and putting away leftovers, something else I hated with a passion. Grandma, as usual, knew exactly what I was up to.

"Weren't you going to ask your father something?" she said, as I slowly stuffed leftover potatoes into an old peanut butter jar.

"I was?" I said, sounding totally surprised. "What?"

"You know what."

"Oh, that," I said, as though I hadn't given it a thought. "Well, I think I'll wait till we finish the dishes."

"Why?"

"I want to finish the dishes first!" I knew how ridiculous that sounded, but she had the grace not to laugh.

"Never saw you so anxious to do dishes before!"

"He's . . . not in a good mood," I said, trying to think of a reason not to ask him.

"Any man's in a good mood once he's had a good meal," said Grandma. She believed that eating would fix just about anything that was wrong with anybody. "That was when I'd always ask your grandpa for things—after supper."

"But Grandpa loved you. I don't think Dad loves me."

"Of course he does!" she said, sounding shocked. "You're his child!"

"He never hugs me or kisses me."

"He ain't very good at showin' how he feels," she said quietly, looking at me to see if I understood.

"When Carla Mae's father gets home, he grabs her up in his arms and twirls her around . . ."

"Your Dad ain't the huggin' kind."

"He'd love me a lot more if I was a boy . . ."

"Now that's a gosh-darned thing to say!" Grandma said, and I knew she was upset, because she never used slang like "gosh-darned."

"Well, he treats me like a boy. He taught me to box! I bet when I was born, he wanted me to be a boy!"

"Your dad and mother waited for you for a long . . . they thought you were the greatest baby in the world!" She shook her head at the memory. "They didn't give a fig whether you were a boy or a girl."

I fidgeted around the table for a moment, clearing dishes, then suddenly changed the subject. "Don't give me a doll or anything like that this Christmas."

"Well, I sure wouldn't," she said. "The way you got all them poor dolls stuffed in the old dresser drawer in the basement, you don't deserve another one."

"I want a pair of cowboy boots."

"Cowboy boots? What for?"

"To wear to school, like Billy Wild."

"Thought you didn't like Billy," she said, giving me an amused look.

"I despise him!" I said haughtily. "But I love his boots."

I went on putting things away. Grandma was not going to let me off the hook.

"That's enough," she said. "I'll finish up."

"I'll dry!"

"No, you go speak to your father."

"Shall I cover this pie with wax paper?"

"I'll do it," she said. "You've got something to ask your father. Go ask him . . ."

"Well, what's all the hurry?" I asked. "Maybe I'll wait and ask him tomorrow."

"Never put off until tomorrow . . ." she started to say.

"I know, I know," I said, nervously hanging onto the back of a chair. "OK, I'm going."

"Go ahead, then."

"OK, OK." I somehow let go of the chair and went into the living room.

Dad was settled in his big chair reading the newspaper. I eyed him surreptitiously to see what mood he was in. It was hard to tell, because, as Grandma had said, he wasn't much on showing his feelings.

There were a lot of things I liked and respected about my father. I liked that he was tall and slender and had slightly gray hair and looked a little like Randolph Scott, who was always the star of cowboy movies. Dad was an expert with his crane and even though he had his hands in machine grease all day, his fingernails were always clean. He could whistle through his teeth, which I never could learn to do. I liked the way he smelled—of To A Wild Rose hair tonic and tobacco and shaving cream and leather. He knew how to fix his own car and he always beat me at cards and anagrams and checkers.

I knew there were things he liked about me too, but we never told any of this to each other. Instead, we waged a constant, subtle war of irritation, sometimes going at each other "like two cats in a sack," as Grandma would say. On those occasions, she would usually be in the middle, trying not to undermine Dad's authority and at the same time, trying to dispense a little justice on my behalf. I never actually kept score, but I think I broke even in the long run.

I thought I would busy myself with something before I approached him. Our living room was so small, though, that whatever I did always seemed to involve everybody else, especially because I was a bit noisy and Dad was the quiet type. There was Grandma's rocking chair, our small sofa, which was my domain, and the writing desk, where we each had drawers of belongings. Dad's drawers were full of receipts and insurance papers; and Grandma's, full of her stubby pencils and writing tablets and her ubiquitous scraps of paper; and mine, full of playing cards and marbles and jacks and other important things of that nature.

I tried not to disturb Dad as I looked through the drawers. I spied my bag of marbles in the back and pulled the drawer way out to get at them. Of course, it dropped with a tremendous clatter, and Dad put down his paper and looked very annoyed.

"I'm sorry," I said meekly.

"You left the paper in a mess again," he said. He liked to have it folded up neatly, just the way it came, and I almost always forgot to do it after I read the comics.

"Sorry, Dad."

He showed me where I had made a mistake on the crossword puzzle too. It didn't seem to be my night, but I saved the situation a little by complimenting him on how much better he was at crossword puzzles than I was. I couldn't tell if it helped or not. He went back to reading, and I got busy with my marbles on the floor. It was so quiet in the living room that every little click of the marbles seemed tremendously loud. I could tell he had stopped reading and was watching me. I deliberately made a couple of sloppy shots.

"No, no," he said, "not like that." He got out of his chair to show me how. I had known he would fall for it.

He spent a few minutes showing me how to get my knuckle flat on the floor for a smooth shot. I already knew, but I figured being sneaky and making him feel good was fair play when I had an important question to ask.

"Play a game with me, Dad?"

"Nope," he said, getting back into his chair. "Going to bed early." He lit a cigarette and tossed the empty package to me. "Here's something for you . . ."

"Thanks," I said, and started to take out the foil to add to

my collection. "Don't know what to use this for . . ." I said, under my breath.

"What?"

"Can't use this to make tree decorations because we don't have a tree."

"Are you starting that again?" he asked.

"Won't you please buy me a tree, Dad? Please? Just a little tree?"

"I've already told you no, and no means no!"

"A tiny tree? That wouldn't cost very much. You spend more on cigarettes in a week than a tree costs! I added it up!"

I could see that had struck a nerve. He was angry.

"Addie! I told you . . ."

"Please! I *implore* you!"

The big word seemed to annoy him rather than impress him.

"You do not need a tree!"

"I do! I do!"

"What for? We're going to Will's."

"It would make this house happy-looking."

"Looks all right to me," he said.

"But it doesn't look like Christmas in here! It doesn't feel like Christmas either," I said, babbling on. "I don't see why I can't have a tree! All the other kids do!"

"You don't have to do everything the other kids do!"

"Why not? It's not like it's doing something bad. Having a tree is a good thing."

"Will you stop pestering me and go to bed?" he said, raising his newspaper in front of his face to shut me out.

"It's not my bedtime yet!" I shouted angrily.

"Addie!"

"Dad, if you'll let me have a tree, I won't ask for another thing for a whole year!"

He put the paper down, disgusted.

"Will you bet me something?" I asked. He was always making bets with me, and sometimes I could win. "If I win I get the tree, and if I lose, I'll never ask you again."

"All right," he said, looking smug. "I'll make you a bet."

"What is it?"

"I'll bet you can't drink a glass full of water."

"The heck I can't," I said excitedly, and ran to the kitchen to get a glass of water. Just to make sure there would be no question of my integrity, I filled a big, tall jelly glass full and carried it carefully back to the living room. Grandma came in and sat in her rocker to watch. I stood by Dad's chair and gulped it down quickly.

"I won!" I said triumphantly.

"I said you had to drink a glass full," he replied.

"I did!"

"Oh, no," he said, laughing. "You drank it empty."

I was so furious I couldn't speak. I wanted to throw the glass at him. Grandma was reading my mind.

"Give me the glass, Addie," she said gently. I handed it to her and ran into our bedroom. I leaned up against the door, shaking with anger. He had been mean and unfair, and there was no way I could get back at him. I hated being a kid at moments like that. I wanted to be grown-up so I could get even.

I could hear Grandma talking to him from the living room.

"James, that was cruel," she said.

"Where's your sense of humor? It was just a joke."

"You wouldn't play a joke like that on one of your friends. What a thing to do to a child, over something she wants so much."

Dad didn't answer. I knew he hated it when Grandma scolded him as though he were still her little boy.

"James," she said quietly. "Let her have a tree this year. It means so much to her. Why not? Have you forgotten what it's like to be ten years old?"

"She has to learn. In this life you can't have everything you want." I could tell from his low voice that he was angry.

"It's Christmas, for goodness' sakes," said Grandma. "A tree's such a small thing to make her happy. You might be surprised at yourself. You might enjoy it too."

"You're one hundred per cent wrong about that."

"You've let your whole life turn sour," said Grandma. "You've no right to sour Addie's life too."

"I don't want to talk about it . . ."

"You don't want nothin' around to remind you. Well, Addie's around. You can't look at her and not be reminded."

I didn't know what they were talking about, but I could tell they were both upset.

"I don't have to listen to this!" he said angrily, and I heard him get up from his chair and start toward the kitchen door.

"For two cents I'd buy her a tree myself," Grandma called after him.

"Don't you do it, Mother!" he said angrily. "She's my

daughter and I'll decide what she can and can't have."

Then I heard him go out and get in his truck and drive away. I had made a mess of things again.

# Chapter Four

I STAYED IN BED late the next morning, making sure Dad had left for work before I got up, so I wouldn't have to face him at breakfast. Then I gulped down my own breakfast quickly and headed across the snowy lawn toward Carla Mae's house next door.

Carla Mae and I always used our special path between the row of poplar trees that separated our yards, and at any time of the day you were likely to see one or both of us come shooting through the trees in mid-air and land with a thud on the lawn. Now, with snow on the ground, and big, clunky overshoes and a heavy coat, and an armload of books, it wasn't easy to make the leap, but I got a running start and landed almost standing up in Carla Mae's yard. I thought of going back and trying it again to see if I could get a better landing, but it was getting late.

I pounded on the back door of the Carters' house with our special knock so Carla Mae would know it was me.

"I'm not ready yet!" I heard her yell from inside, so I went in to wait for her.

She was in the kitchen finishing up her breakfast, and the place was in its usual uproar. Her four-year-old sister, Debbie, was standing on a chair in front of the stove, frying an egg for her own breakfast. Minnie, their fat, black Scottie, was sitting on another chair at the table and finishing up somebody's left-over sausage. Two-year-old Tim came waddling through in his diaper, with his bottle firmly clenched in his teeth, and several other people of assorted sizes and shapes were in and out of chairs and under the table and all over the kitchen. The table was a hodgepodge of half-eaten food, three-wheeled trucks, one-eyed dolls and broken crayons, all in happy confusion. Carla Mae grabbed one last piece of sausage before Minnie could get to it, and pulled on her coat.

As we left I thought how different her family was from mine and how they seemed to be able to understand each other so much better than we did. I was feeling very depressed by the time we got into the school cloakroom and started struggling out of our heavy coats and galoshes. Then Jerry Walsh made a crack about my grandmother, and that was the last straw. I clunked him right over the head with one of my wet galoshes, and a real fight got started.

Miss Thompson was there immediately.

"Stop that at once!" she said, and pulled us apart.

"She hit me first," said Jerry in his whiny voice.

"You asked for it!" I said.

"He started it!" Carla Mae said, coming to my rescue. "He was making fun of her grandmother."

"I was not," said Jerry.

"You were so!" I answered.

"It's not my fault your grandmother's an old character!" he said.

"She is not a character!" I shouted.

"She looks like a nut, pulling that little red wagon!"

"It's my wagon, and she can pull it any damn time she wants!"

"Addie!" said Miss Thompson sternly. "There will be no swearing here."

"She takes my wagon to the grocery store," I explained to Miss Thompson. "She's too old to carry big, heavy bags."

"Yeah," said Jerry, snickering. "And when she wants Addie to come home she sticks her head out the window and blows a police whistle!"

"Sounds like a good system to me," said Miss Thompson.

"It's nutty!" said Jimmy.

"Say that once more, and I'll punch you in the nose!" I snarled.

"Now, calm down, Addie," said Miss Thompson with her hand on my shoulder. "You children don't seem to know the difference between a 'nut' and a 'character.' Come inside the classroom, and we'll talk about it."

She started into the room with the others, and Jerry and I lingered behind, both hoping to get in the last word.

"You sure got up on the wrong side of the bed, you grump!" he said.

"You better button your lip, creep!" I hissed at him, hands on my hips. "I dare you to say one more thing to me."

At that moment, Miss Thompson looked back to see what we were doing, and motioned us both to come into the room. We did, and I had the last word.

Miss Thompson talked to us about "nuts" and "characters," and we all came to the conclusion that a nut was someone who was crazy, while a character was just someone who was different, like Thoreau or Columbus, and not a bad thing to be at all.

After our discussion, we practiced Christmas carols for the caroling we were going to do that night, and I had a sudden inspiration as we practiced. I told them that when we stopped at my house I wanted them to sing a certain carol that was my grandmother's favorite. The class agreed and we practiced it. I wondered how it would go over at home.

After school that afternoon, our committee for buying Miss Thompson's present trooped uptown to Main Street to do our shopping. The class had had the good sense to elect four girls— no boys, thank heavens—so I knew we would be able to choose something nice. Boys were so dippy to go shopping with. They always giggled and acted crazy if you tried to pick out something personal like bubble bath or dusting powder, and the year before there were boys on the committee, and they were going to buy Miss Thompson a horrible, dowdy wool shawl. They simply didn't understand glamour and good taste, and we had no use for them on a shopping trip. I don't think they minded at all.

The committee got into three separate snowball fights on the way uptown and had to stop and talk to a lot of people. It was one of those towns where you knew who lived in every house and recognized every car and said hello to everyone on the street. There was one doctor, one movie theatre, and five bars and five churches, which the people of Clear River found a nice balance of sin and salvation. We also had a weekly town newspaper, where it was big news if Mrs. Dinsley wallpapered her upstairs bedroom.

We decided to try shopping at the drugstore first, because Mr. Brady always had a good selection of gifts. We passed the IGA grocery on the way, and while the other girls went on ahead, I peeked at the price tags on the Christmas trees standing outside on the sidewalk. I was hoping that, since Christmas was so near, the prices might be reduced, but I saw that the trees were still too expensive for me to buy one from my allowance, especially after my Christmas shopping.

Our gift-buying committee looked at just about everything Mr. Brady had in the whole drugstore and couldn't agree on anything. I said I was nearly ready to give up and give Miss Thompson something practical like nose drops, and Tanya Smithers said that was the most disgusting thing she had ever heard of. I wanted to say, "Wait till you see the icky gloves I got for you," but I didn't. I didn't want to spoil the surprise.

Mr. Brady suggested Evening in Paris cologne.

"She buys that all the time," he said.

"We know," said Carla Mae. We knew a lot of such details about Miss Thompson, because we came right out and asked her.

"We don't want to give her stuff she buys herself!" I said, annoyed at everyone's lack of imagination. We turned down a comb and brush set and a manicure set and bubble bath and a brooch shaped like a Christmas tree. Mr. Brady's suggestion of a curling iron just made us laugh, because we all knew Miss Thompson had naturally curly hair. I explained to Mr. Brady that that was why her hair style looked like Betty Grable's.

We told him we had four dollars and twenty-five cents to spend, and he said he thought he had something we might like, though it was a bit expensive. Then he got a box down from a high shelf and brought out the most beautiful thing we had ever seen—a fabulous jewelry box made of deep blue mirror-glass.

"Zowie!" I said. "That looks like something a real movie star would have on her dresser!"

"Yeah," sighed Carla Mae. "Betty Grable would like that!"

Mr. Brady lifted the lid, and the box began to play "The Blue Danube." We all stared at it goggle-eyed. It was lined with pale blue velvet. We wanted it.

"How much is it?" I asked, afraid to hear the answer.

Mr. Brady turned the price tag over, and I saw that it read $5.95. I started to tell him we couldn't afford it when he pulled out a pencil and crossed out the $5.95 and wrote in $4.25.

"Been meaning to put this thing on sale for some time now," he said. "Glad I remembered to do it in time for Christmas." We all smiled at him, and he smiled back, and we took the box and carried it very carefully home and wrapped it.


After supper, we met to go caroling, and in a half-hour we came by my house, where Grandma was making hot chocolate for us. We all came into the kitchen, stomping the snow off our boots and unwrapping our mufflers. As soon as we could get out of our boots, we all went into the living room, blew our noses and got ready to sing. I stepped forward and said, "Now we're going to sing a special request." I didn't say it was Grandma's special request, as I had told the class. In fact, it wasn't her request at all.

Dad was settled in his chair, and Grandma in her rocker as we began to sing. When Dad heard the first strains of "Oh,

Christmas Tree," he looked at me suspiciously, and I looked away. He knew what I was up to. We sang every verse, and it took quite a while. When I got up the courage, I looked over at Dad again, and I saw that he had a very sad look on his face and seemed to be far away somewhere, lost in his thoughts. I wondered if singing "Oh, Christmas Tree" had been such a good idea after all.

# Chapter Five

THE NEXT MORNING at breakfast, Dad, Grandma and I were careful not to mention the words "Christmas" or "tree" to each other. We seemed to have made a momentary truce, and breakfast was proceeding as usual. Dad was telling me a lot of things I didn't think were important, about sitting up straight and getting your elbows off the table, and I was telling him a lot of things he didn't think were important, about what we were going to do at school that day, and Grandma wasn't paying any attention to either of us because she was trying to get a pancake all the way from the stove to the table without putting it on a plate. She would pick it up from the skillet with her spatula and then whirl around and try to get it to land on somebody's plate instead of on the floor. Sometimes it worked and sometimes it didn't.

Grandma always did everything the hard way, which was just her nature. She would rather risk dropping the pancakes than dirty another dish. She saw that as her kind of individualism, but my dad found it very irritating, and I thought it was just plain funny. The three of us seldom had the same reaction to anything. As I look back on it now, I see that our differences had a lot to do with enriching my life, but at the age of ten, I saw them only as the cause of all my troubles.

A pancake hit the floor just then, and Grandma gave a little snort of a laugh and stomped her foot on the floor as though to punish herself for missing the target.

"Whoopsie!" she said, and flung the fallen pancake halfway across the kitchen and into the sink. My dad always said she would have been a heck of a shortstop, but this morning he didn't find her slapdash way of doing things very amusing.

"If you don't hit my plate with one of those pretty soon," he said, "I'll have to leave for work without my breakfast."

"Here, Dad, you can have one of mine," I said, and started to scrape one off my plate onto his.

"No!" said Dad, and quickly put his hand protectively over his plate. "I wouldn't touch one of those with a shovel. The way you eat, Addie, you'll be lucky if you live past ten."

That was his clever way of saying that he didn't approve of what I put on my pancakes—peanut butter and jelly.

"I'm the tallest person in the fifth grade, so I guess I'm eating OK," I said. "And there's really no reason why a person shouldn't put peanut butter and jelly on pancakes. After all, they're made of flour, just like bread, and you put peanut butter and jelly on bread, don't you?"

"I don't! And I don't want any lectures on what pancakes are made of either. I've been eating them all my life. When I can get 'em, that is," he said, and looked meaningfully at Grandma.

"Comin' up!" shouted Grandma, like a short order cook, and spun around and shot one in the direction of his plate. It landed half on his plate and half on the oilcloth, and she looked quite satisfied with that. Dad just shook his head silently and slid the pancake onto his plate, and I pressed my lips together hard to keep from laughing.

After Dad left for work, Grandma managed to aim a couple of pancakes at her own plate and sat down at the table. I took my plate to the sink, and she noticed for the first time what I was wearing—my usual costume of jeans and red flannel cowboy shirt with green piping around the collar. I had put green rubber bands on my pigtails to match the green trim on my shirt, and I thought that was Christmasy enough for anybody the last day before Christmas vacation. Grandma didn't agree.

"You're not going to school like that the last day before vacation!" she said. "This is the day you open presents in your class. You ought to wear something good. Go put on your red plaid circle skirt and red sweater."

I knew from experience I would never win an argument about clothes with Grandma, so I groaned a lot and dragged myself into our bedroom and changed. I hated wearing skirts because I had to wear old-fashioned heavy cotton stockings that were held up by a horrid garter belt.

In the wintertime, Grandma always made me wear "snuggies" and warm cotton undershirts, and when they were combined with garters and long stockings, I felt miserably uncomfortable and tied up. I was gangly and skinny, and I hated having my knobby knees sticking out from under my skirt. Besides, it was cold. I made a horrible face at myself in the mirror as I dressed.

I finally got into the whole get-up, right down to my sturdy brown oxfords, which I wore every day. I was never allowed to wear tennis shoes or penny loafers or, what I wanted most of all, cowboy boots, because they would "ruin" my feet. The only other shoes I had besides my sturdy oxfords were my black patent leather Mary Janes, which I wore to church on Sunday. Then I had to take them off right away when I got home, because even Mary Janes would ruin my feet.

I never knew why so much time was spent worrying about feet, except that my father had been rejected by the army in World War I because he had flat feet. When he went back to school, he was the only boy left in the class, and he had been so embarrassed that he dropped out in the eleventh grade. I, however, didn't plan to go into the army, so I didn't see what difference it made if my arches were high up or flat as a pancake. But then, grownups always had a lot of strange ideas. At the shoe store in Omaha, the man put your foot in a weird machine, and then you looked down through a scope of some sort, and in the middle of this screen filled with green light, you could see the bones of your foot—your own foot skeleton wiggling around—and the man could tell you if your feet were getting ruined and if you needed a bigger size this year. I seemed to need a bigger size about every six months.

Carla Mae arrived just as I finished dressing, and we went into the living room to make the Christmas card that would go with Miss Thompson's fabulous blue glass jewelry box. I drew a sleigh and reindeer, and Carla Mae watched.

"I just don't know how you do it," she said. "You're really good."

"I don't know how I do it either," I said. "It just comes out." I had never been able to figure out why I could draw and other people couldn't. I found it very mysterious, but I was grateful that I could.

"Should we put 'For Miss Thompson' or 'For Sylvia Thompson'?"

"Miss," said Carla Mae, always mindful of propriety.

"How about 'Miss Sylvia Thompson'?" I said, not wanting to be too stuffy. Carla Mae nodded.

"Boy, I wish my name was Sylvia," I said.

"How come?"

"I hate the name Adelaide . . . and Addie! Yuck! When I grow up, I'm going to change my name!"

"You can't change your name!"

"You can do anything you want when you're grown up."

"I'm going to wear a long, white dress and a veil," she said dreamily. "And get married."

"Well, I'm going to be a painter and live in Paris, France, and *never* get married!"

Carla Mae gave me a disgusted look. I always wondered how we could be such good friends when we had such different daydreams for ourselves.

We were all restless that day in school, waiting for the gift exchange in the afternoon. Finally, the moment arrived. Delmer Doakes put on the Santa beard and hat we had made for him in art class and began to distribute the gifts. As he took each gift from under the tree, he would call out the person's name and that person would go to the front of the room, read the tag, open the gift and show it to everyone. There was a lot of giggling and groaning over ugly gifts and dumb gifts and gifts between boys and girls who didn't like each other and even more giggling over those who did. Then Delmer called Tanya's name.

She went up and took the gift from him and read the tag. "Merry Christmas to Tanya Smithers from Adelaide Mills." Carla Mae and I exchanged evil glances.

Tanya tore open the package, and with an expression of great distaste, drew out the ugly brown wool gloves I had found at the Clear River Variety Store. The whole class snickered and groaned, well aware that I had deliberately given her an icky present. She was aware of it too.

"Thanks!" she said sarcastically, and sat down.

Delmer called my name next, and I went up and was handed a tiny box. When I saw who had drawn my name, I turned bright red.

"Merry Christmas and Happy New Year, to Adelaide Mills," I read, "From Billy Wild." Everybody snickered. They were always teasing Billy and me about liking each other. I opened the little box, and there inside was something absolutely horrifying. I stood there looking at it until Miss Thompson said, "Hold it up Addie, so everyone can see."

I flashed it quickly in front of the class, hoping they wouldn't see what it was, but they all howled, and I turned from red to purple and sat down quickly. Horrible Billy had given me a heart-shaped locket! In front of the whole class! I shoved the box down into the pocket of my cardigan and silently swore that I would never speak to him again.

Delmer called Miss Thompson's name next, and I was thankful the attention turned from me.

"What a beautiful card," she said, when she saw it. "I'll bet

I know who made it." That compliment took my mind off my embarrassment, and then she unwrapped the blue box. Everyone gasped when she took it out, and when she lifted the lid and it began to play "The Blue Danube," the class broke into applause.

Miss Thompson said it was certainly the nicest and most tasteful present she had ever received, and we all applauded ourselves again.

Carla Mae and I were busy whispering about what a great choice of gifts we had made when I heard Miss Thompson ask who didn't have a Christmas tree at home. I didn't know why she was asking, but I put my hand up before I realized how embarrassing it would be. Surely I was the only one, and everyone spotted my hand before I could get it down, and I turned crimson. Then I realized that there was another hand up. It was Gloria Cott, from the only poor family in town. I knew they had no money, but I was surprised that the Cotts were really too poor to buy a Christmas tree. My reason, after all, was just some stubborn quirk of my father's, but I was afraid everyone would think we were poor too. Miss Thompson looked surprised to see my hand raised, and I wondered what she thought.

"As you know," said Miss Thompson, "we usually leave all the school Christmas trees up during vacation and then have a big bonfire on the playground when we come back from vacation, but this year I thought it would be better to give our tree to someone who doesn't have one at home. Since there are two people . . . I guess we'll choose a number between one and ten, and the closest will take the tree home."

I felt a surge of excitement, and I knew right then that I was going to win the tree. Dad had taught me how to play the odds on choosing between one and ten, and I was sure I had a better chance than Gloria.

Gloria chose first and chose 8, and I knew she didn't know how to play the odds. I chose 7. I wasn't even surprised when Miss Thompson said the number was 5, and I had won. I couldn't take my eyes off the tree for the rest of the afternoon.

# Chapter Six

CARLA MAE STAYED AFTER SCHOOL with me to help remove the decorations from the tree before taking it home.

"You sure were lucky," she said, as we worked.

"It wasn't luck. I know how to play the odds. Dad taught me."

"How?"

"If you go first, you always choose 5 or 6, so you get at least half the numbers on the high side or low side. If you go second, you choose the number right next to the other player's, so at least you get all the numbers higher or lower than his, whichever gives you the most numbers. Get it?"

"No," said Carla Mae, annoyed.

"Look, Gloria guessed 8, so all I had to do was guess 7, and that meant I had all the numbers from 1 to 7 and she only had 8, 9 and 10. So my odds were 7 to 3."

"But you could have guessed 9, then she would have won!"

"I just explained why I didn't guess 9!"

"You mean you were lucky?"

"Oh, no," I groaned, and started to write it all down for her on the blackboard. "You're just no good at gambling!"

We finally got the tree undecorated, and Carla Mae helped

me drag it home through the snow. We struggled up the porch steps and through the door with it, and strained to lift it upright on its wooden base. When we had it up, we collapsed on the sofa and sat there admiring it. My heart was pounding.

"Doesn't it look nifty?" Carla Mae asked.

"Looks OK," I said, sounding bored. "I didn't really care whether I won it or not, but since I won it, it looks OK."

"It's almost up to the ceiling," she said, looking around the small room.

"Not bad for a free tree," I said.

Just then Grandma came into the room to see what we were doing. When she saw the tree, she stopped dead in her tracks and looked stunned.

"It's from school!" I said excitedly, running over to her. "We guessed numbers from one to ten, and I won!"

"Your dad is goin' to have a fit!" she said.

"Why? It didn't cost anything!"

"That's not the point," said Grandma. "My glory, it's a beauty! Must be seven, maybe eight foot."

"Why won't Dad like it?" I asked.

"Maybe it'll be all right," Grandma said, but she sounded as though she didn't really think so. "We'll wait and see when he comes home. Now get those boots off, you two, snow's meltin' all over the rug!"

Soon Carla Mae and I were sprawled out on the living room rug, cutting paper decorations for the tree. We made colored chains, snowflakes, stars, circles, candles, bells and tiny Christmas tree shapes, colored them and put glitter on them. Then we drew a five-pointed star on cardboard, carefully cut it out and covered it with tin foil I had been saving from gum wrappers and Dad's cigarette packages.

We asked Grandma to come in and fasten the star on top of the tree, because I knew her strong old fingers could bend a hairpin tighter around the top branch than ours could. We held a chair for her to climb on.

"Oh, glory!" she exclaimed. "You expect me to get up there with my rheumatism? I'll get dizzy."

"No, you won't," I assured her. "We'll hold you up."

Carla Mae looked at her moccasins as she climbed up on the chair. "Do you wear those because you're a 'character'?" she asked Grandma.

Grandma looked down at her. "Who says I'm a character?"

"Miss Thompson," replied Carla Mae.

"She did, did she?" said Grandma, looking puzzled. "How'd Miss Thompson happen to say that?"

"A character's a good thing to be!" I said quickly, not wanting her to misunderstand. "It means somebody like . . . Columbus . . . who does what other people are afraid to do, and doesn't give a fig if they laugh at him!"

"How come Miss Thompson was hookin' me up to Columbus?" asked Grandma as she took a hairpin out of her hair and used it to wire the star to the top of the tree.

"Some kid was making fun of you, so Addie punched him!" Carla Mae blurted out. I gave her a dirty look.

"Got yourself into another fight, did you?" asked Grandma.

I nodded.

"Well, good for you!" she said. "Glad your dad taught you to box." I was surprised at her enthusiasm. She finished with the star. "There!" she said.

"That looks nifty, Grandma. Thank you." We helped her down. "When I grow up, I'm going to be a character too," I said. "So's Carla Mae."

"I am?" asked Carla Mae, looking very unsure.

Just then I heard Dad's pickup in the driveway.

"He's home!" I said, and Carla Mae leaped across the room and grabbed her coat.

"I gotta go!" she shouted, and was out the door before I could even say good-bye. I knew she didn't want to be there for the fireworks that were about to happen.

I went nervously to the kitchen with Grandma, and we waited for Dad. He came in and put his lunch bucket on the table, as he did every night, and I opened it to see if there was anything left, as I did every night. I grabbed a cupcake and started to chomp at it nervously, as he went toward the living room. Grandma and I both watched the door apprehensively. For a moment there was nothing but silence.

Then he shouted, "Where the hell did that come from?"

"I won it!" I said excitedly, and ran into the living room, with Grandma following right behind me.

Dad was standing there frozen, looking at the tree with a painful expression on his face.

"I won it by figuring out the odds on a number between one and ten!" I went on. "Just the way you taught me! Miss Thompson asked who didn't have a tree, and Gloria Cott and I raised our hands, and . . ."

"Gloria Cott?" he said.

"Yes . . ."

"You think we're like the Cotts? Think I take charity, do you?" he shouted.

"No, Dad, it's just that Gloria and I were the only ones who didn't have a tree . . ."

"Then why didn't she take it home!"

"I told you, I won it! Because you taught me how to figure odds . . . so Carla Mae and I carried it home."

"Dragged it through the streets—letting the whole town think we take cast-offs—like some bums!"

"James," said Grandma, "that tree's not hurtin' anything."

"I do not take charity!" he shouted at her.

"It's not charity," said Grandma firmly. "She won it fair and square."

"If I want a tree, I can damn well buy it myself!" he said.

"She's the one who wants it," Grandma said, "not you."

"She has to learn she can't have everything she wants, not in this life," he said angrily. "I don't have anything I want. Do you think I like working a crane fifty weeks a year? I'd like to go somewhere and sit in the sun and forget both of you!"

I had never heard Dad say anything like that about Grandma and me, and I began to cry and ran into the bedroom and closed the door. I could hear them in the living room, still arguing.

"I want that tree out of my house!" he shouted at Grandma.

"It's my house, James, and I say the tree can stay right where it is!"

I knew then that this was no ordinary argument. Grandma had never thrown it up to Dad that we were living in her house.

I knew she had said something very serious in sticking up for me, and I was scared.

"If you don't want me here, I'll be glad to move out and take Addie with me," he said, trying to get back at her.

"Don't talk nonsense!"

"I'm telling you, Mother, if we stay here, I'm not having you interfere between me and my daughter!"

"She's more than your daughter," said Grandma, trying to calm him down. "She's a human being. She's got feelings, even if you haven't. James, don't you see—the last person you felt anything for was Helen."

"Leave her out of it!" he said angrily. Dad never liked to talk about my mother very much, and I was surprised that Grandma would even bring it up.

"I know you were brokenhearted," she said. "But you're not the only man who's ever lost a wife. It's almost ten years! That kind of grief is selfish. That child needs your love."

"I proved I loved her, didn't I?" he asked. "I wouldn't let Will and Nora take her to live with them. I kept her. I took the responsibility."

"While she was a baby it was all right," Grandma said. "You could carry her around like a doll, plop her in her crib when you didn't feel like carryin' her, chuck her under the chin. She was just a cute baby. Now she's growin' into a person, and you don't know what to do with her! You hold yourself away and live in this house like a stranger. When she's old enough, she's going to leave you, James. Then you won't have the responsibility, and you won't have a daughter, either."

I had never heard Grandma talk that way to Dad, and when

she had finished, neither of them said any more for a few moments. Finally he spoke.

"It was my fault," he said quietly. "Having the baby is what killed her."

"It was pneumonia, son," Grandma said gently.

"People don't have to die of pneumonia. It was the baby that weakened her. If she hadn't had the baby. It was all because of me."

"No, James," Grandma said softly. "You both wanted a baby. It wasn't your fault, or Addie's. It just happened. No good ever comes of layin' blame."

Neither of them said any more then, and I heard him get up and go into his bedroom and close the door.

# Chapter Seven

BY THE TIME Grandma and I went to bed that night, I was sorry I had brought the tree home. I was beginning to feel guilty about Gloria Cott not having a tree—"the poor souls," Grandma always called the Cott family. And I was sorry I had ever raised my hand in class. I shouldn't have let anyone know that my dad wouldn't buy a Christmas tree. There was something very bad about it, and it was going to ruin our whole Christmas.

I crawled into the old four-poster bed and huddled up between the freezing sheets. Grandma was always warm, even on the coldest nights, and I loved to sleep with her because she let me put my cold feet on her warm legs. Whenever I had to cry over something, it almost always happened at that time of the night. Being close to Grandma in bed gave me some sense of freedom and relief, and whatever had hurt me during the day usually came out then. Sometimes she could help me with my problems and sometimes not, but she always held on to me, and that made me feel I could get through it. That night I cried and cried.

"How long you goin' to cry?" she asked softly.

"I don't know. Maybe all night!" I said, still sobbing.

"Don't you worry, he'll get over it," she said.

"He's so mean . . ."

"He's not mean," Grandma said. "Jamie's a good man."

"Jamie?"

"That's what we called him when he was a boy. He was proud then too. He always had a lot of pride."

"What's so great about pride?"

"It's a way of . . . of thinkin' well of yourself. You've got it. That's why you hit that kid today."

"Was that pride?"

"You were stickin' up for me because you love me, and I'm your family. Your father insists on payin' our way because he loves us, and we're his family. He's always been the kind who wouldn't take nothin' from nobody, even if we were starvin'. Ten, fifteen years ago, during the Depression, we had a bad time."

"What was the Depression?"

"Wasn't any jobs. Nobody had any money. Lots of people had to go on charity. Your father wouldn't even take the flour or the potatoes the government was handing out free."

"Would Dad have let you starve?"

"Of course not. But he was pretty stubborn about acceptin' anything he hadn't earned. Wouldn't take charity."

"When you take a present, like a Christmas present," I asked, "is that charity?"

"No," Grandma said. "That's a whole different thing. A gift is somethin' from someone who wants to make you happy."

"He doesn't love me!" I said, starting to cry again. "He just doesn't love me!"

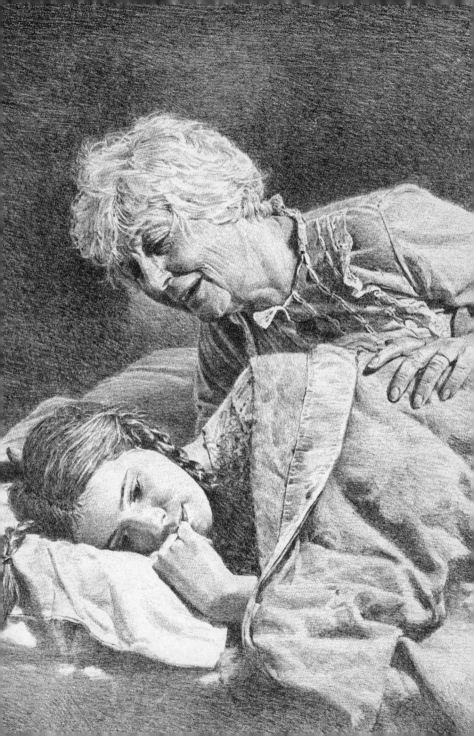

"Hush, now, I'm not listening to such talk! The truth is," she said quietly, "your dad hasn't wanted a Christmas tree in this house because it reminds him of your momma and your first Christmas with the three of you together, and it makes him feel bad."

"I didn't know that."

"He misses her an awful lot."

"You mean the tree made him unhappy?"

"Maybe," she said, "but it's not your fault. Someday he'll get over it, and things will be all right. Think you can go to sleep now?"

I nodded my head, and Grandma hugged me close. I tried to go to sleep, but my mind wouldn't shut off.

I lay there for a long while and tried to remember my mother, but I couldn't. All I knew about her were the things I found in her scrapbook and the snapshots in the family album. My father never talked about her. I tried to remember my first Christmas, but I couldn't remember that either. I wondered if my father had gone into his bedroom and cried when he saw the tree. It scared me to think of him being so upset over something that I didn't even know about.

I thought more about just what charity meant and about my father and about Gloria Cott. After a while, when I heard Grandma snoring, I quietly moved away from her across the icy sheets. There were so many heavy quilts and comforters on the bed that I could hardly make my way to the edge of it. Finally I managed to worm my way out from under the covers, and when my bare feet touched the painfully cold wooden floor, I wanted to scream.

I tiptoed to our closet and slipped into socks and pulled a sweater on over my pajama tops. Then I sneaked into the living room and carefully tipped the tree down to the floor. I thought about taking off the decorations, but I knew I had no time to waste. I found some paper and a pencil in the writing desk, wrote a note and struggled into my boots and coat. I unlocked the front door and opened it slowly. It let out a groan like the creaking door on the opening of the "Inner Sanctum" mystery show.

I eased the tree out onto the porch, and the frozen snow crunched under my feet. I was sure Dad would wake up. His bedroom window overlooked the porch, and he always slept with the window open a bit, even in the dead of winter. I recalled every cowboy movie I had ever seen, and tried to remember how the Indians had crept silently up on the settlers. After what seemed like an hour, I had eased the tree down off the porch steps and onto the lawn, the frozen snow making explosive cracks with every step I took.

I had never been out alone at this hour, and I was a little frightened. It was after midnight, the dead of night for Clear River, and there wasn't a house light on or a car in sight, only the distant sound of trains and the occasional bark of a dog. There were big dogs in the neighborhood, and they ran loose. I didn't know if they could see in the dark the way cats could. What if they mistook me for a burglar?

I was glad it was only a block to Gloria's house. I slowly dragged the tree down the snowy sidewalk and across the Cott's lawn and propped it up against their rickety porch railing. Then I pulled the note I had written out of my pocket and stuck it onto the tree. It read, "To Gloria, From Santa Claus."

# Chapter Eight

THE NEXT MORNING when I heard Grandma and Dad in the kitchen, I stayed in bed, afraid of another explosion when they found the tree gone. Grandma was so preoccupied with fixing breakfast that she hadn't gone into the living room yet, and hadn't noticed the tree was missing. Finally I heard Dad go into the living room. For a moment there was silence, then he went back into the kitchen.

"What did you do with the tree?" he asked Grandma.

"What?"

"When did you take it down?" he asked.

"I didn't take it down," she said, and she went in to see for herself. "Oh, dear! Addie must have done it. You had her so upset. I told her it made you feel bad because it reminded you of Helen. I guess I shouldn't have done that."

I heard him coming toward the bedroom. He opened the door and called to me to wake up. I pretended to be asleep and finally rubbed my eyes and rolled over.

"What did you do with that tree?" he asked.

"I gave it away."

"You what?"

"I gave it away to Gloria Cott, because they don't have one."

"When?"

"Last night, when everybody was asleep."

He looked at me as though I were crazy. I thought he was going to yell at me for being out alone at night, but he said nothing.

"I didn't wake anybody up," I went on. "I just put it on their porch and put a note on it that said, 'From Santa Claus' so they wouldn't be mad that it was charity."

He looked out my bedroom window, toward the Cott's house down the block.

"It's not there now," he said.

I looked too. "I bet they got up early and found it!" I said.

"That's the damndest thing I ever heard of," he said, and went back into the kitchen and closed the door.

He told Grandma what I had done, and then he left for work. I was afraid now that he was so angry he might not even let us go to Uncle Will's house for Christmas. Maybe Will's tree reminded him of my mother too.

The Christmas pageant was that night, and after supper we all raced around getting ready. I had to put on warm clothes under my angel costume and find a way of carrying my cardboard wings so they wouldn't get bent.

Grandma was getting all dressed up, and I had to help with her shoes. When she dressed up, she wore high-heeled shoes with straps and buckles on them. She could never see the tiny holes to buckle them, and it was always my job to get down on the floor on my knees and fasten them for her. I would try one hole, and then she would throw her leg up in the air and wiggle her ankle around to determine if that was too tight or too loose, and then put it down for further adjustments, if necessary.

Finally we were ready and we all piled into the pickup for the quick drive to the church. On the way we passed the Cott's house, and we could see the schoolroom tree in their tiny living room. All the kids were putting paper ornaments on it, and at the top, still wired securely on, was the star Carla Mae and I had made.

"Sure looks nice, don't it?" Grandma whispered to me as we passed, and I knew Dad had heard her. He didn't say a word, and neither did I. I vowed I would never mention a tree in front of him again.

When we got to the church, I met Carla Mae and the others backstage, and we milled around and whispered while the pageant began and we waited to make our entrances as angels and the animals in the manger scene. I could hear Billy Wild out on the stage, doing the narration, while everyone else shuffled on and off on cue.

Someone dressed as a cow approached Carla Mae and me.

"Who's that?" I asked.

"It's me—Gloria," she said, and took off her cow mask.

"I didn't even recognize you! That's a really great costume!"

"Yours too," she said.

"Yeah. My dad says I'm miscast as an angel, though."

The three of us laughed.

"Guess what we have, Addie? A tree!" Gloria said. "Santa Claus brought it."

We smiled at each other, and I knew she had guessed where it came from.

"You're wearing your locket!" Gloria said, looking at the front of my costume.

I quickly covered it with my hand, embarrassed. "Oh, I was just trying it on. I forgot I was wearing it!"

She and Carla Mae giggled, and the three of us sat around whispering, waiting to go on. We took off our shoes to rub our feet, trying to keep warm in the drafty halls of the church, when Carla Mae and I got the bright idea of tying the toes of our long, heavy stockings together. We were both wearing our horrible garter belts, and we stretched our stockings at the toes until we had enough fabric to tie her left toe to my right toe and vice versa. Then we stood up and hopped around like a crazy, four-legged thing with wings and halos.

At just that moment, Miss Thompson came in and told us it was time to go on. We nearly panicked when we discovered that we couldn't untie the toes of our stockings. They had pulled into knots while we were jumping around, and now the knots wouldn't budge.

"Well, let the cow through!" Miss Thompson said, and she motioned us to sit down on the floor. Then Carla Mae and I stuck our feet up in the air, and Miss Thompson worked frantically on the knots. She finally untied us, and only then did it occur to all of us that we simply could have unhooked our garters and removed our stockings.

We quickly ran on stage as the stage manager let the big star of Bethlehem plunge into the scene, and we waved our cardboard wings and I made the "Fear not, for behold, I bring you good tidings . . ." speech. As I moved toward Billy Wild, at the side of the stage, I suddenly realized that he was staring at the locket, and I slapped my hand over it. I managed to keep one wing waving as I finished my speech.

I could see Grandma and Dad in the audience, and I gave them a little wave. Grandma waved back, and in the half-darkness, I thought I saw Dad smile.

# Chapter Nine

THE NEXT AFTERNOON after lunch, Grandma and I started our annual Christmas project—baking dozens of gingerbread men. My special job was to decorate them after they came out of the oven. We talked as we worked.

"That was a wonderful thing you did with the tree, Addie," she said.

"Oh, well," I said philosophically, "I'm too grown up for trees. Trees are for little kids, like Gloria's brothers and sisters."

"Can't be a very good Christmas at their house, poor souls, him out of work and all."

"She doesn't know how to figure out the odds the way I do, so she'd never have won it," I said.

"I know."

"The only way for her to get a tree was for me to give it to her."

"I'm sure you made her real happy," said Grandma. "I never got around to askin' you—how'd Tanya Smithers like her gloves?"

"She hated them!" I said gleefully. "I knew she would!"

"Call that Christmas spirit?" Grandma asked disapprovingly.

"Tanya Smithers is my worst friend in the fifth grade. I don't want to give her something she'd like!"

"Oughta be ashamed of yourself," said Grandma, trying not to smile. "Who got your name?"

"I'm not telling."

"Was it a boy or a girl?" she asked. "Someone you like or don't like?"

I shook my head silently. I wasn't going to tell even Grandma about the horrible, embarrassing locket from Billy.

"Did he give you a present you like or don't like?"

"How do you know it was a he?" I asked.

"Was it a she?"

"No more questions," I said firmly. "I'm not going to talk about it."

Then Grandma put her hand in her apron pocket, and walked over to the table where I was working. She brought her hand out of her pocket and dangled Billy's locket in front of me.

I grabbed it quickly out of her hand. "You looked in my private drawer!"

"Nobody looks in anybody else's private drawer in this house, Addie."

"Oh, I know where you found it," I said, turning crimson with embarrassment.

"Under your pillow," she said, nodding her head.

"I meant to hide it this morning, but . . ."

"You've had a lot of things on your mind," she said, smiling. "Besides, it sure wasn't hidden last night at the pageant. Sparkled like a star itself up there, even with you fussin' around tryin' to cover it up!"

I opened my hand and looked at it again. "Isn't it disgusting?"

"I think it's real pretty," she said. "From Billy Wild?"

"How did you guess that?" I asked, more embarrassed than ever.

"Because I'm a smart old character!"

"I'm never going to wear this disgusting thing again as long as I live!"

"Why not!"

"If I wear it again, he'll really think I like him!"

"Guess he likes *you* all right," said Grandma.

"Ha!" I said derisively. "How do you know?"

"Wouldn't give a heart locket to a person he didn't like," she said, matter-of-factly. "You like him a little too . . ."

"I've told you a thousand times I despise him!" I said angrily. "I won't even speak to him!"

"Mmmmmmm," said Grandma.

"What do you mean, 'Mmmmm'?"

"Some people don't speak much. Doesn't mean they don't feel anything."

I thought about that for a minute as I finished another row of gingerbread men. Finally the delicious aroma got the best of me, and I chose one to eat.

"Doesn't he look just like Billy Wild?" I asked Grandma, as I held the little man up in front of me.

"Yes," she laughed, "I guess he does a bit."

"Good!" I said. "I'm going to bite his head off and chew him up!"

"Glory, Addie!" she said, laughing.

"What's so funny?"

"I pity the fella you really fall for some day," she said. "He'll be black and blue before he realizes that's your way of likin'. Heavens! It's all right to let on you like people, if you do!"

I looked at her skeptically, then picked up the gingerbread man and bit his head off.

We had almost finished decorating all the gingerbread men when I heard Dad's truck in the driveway. Instead of coming in through the kitchen door as he usually did, he walked slowly around to the front door.

"Addie, open the door!" he shouted, pounding on the door.

I couldn't imagine what was going on, and I ran into the living room and pulled the front door open. I couldn't see Dad at all—the whole doorway was filled with a huge Christmas tree. He pushed it inside and shoved some boxes of ornaments toward me.

"Don't stand there," he said, in his usual impatient manner. "Help me."

I was speechless.

"Careful, now," he said, as I took the boxes. "Those are breakable."

Grandma came into the room, and stopped, staring at the tree. "Oh, James!" she said softly.

"If we're going to have a Christmas tree, we can buy it ourselves."

"Isn't it beautiful!" said Grandma, coming over and putting her hand on my shoulder. I just stood there holding the boxes, frozen to the spot.

Grandma took the boxes from me. "Oh, look, Addie. Decorations—silver icicles and lights!"

Dad was setting up the tree at the end of the room, and I finally came out of my daze and looked down at the boxes I was holding.

"Is there a star?" I asked.

"Oh, James," said Grandma. "You forgot to get a star."

"The one I made is still on the other tree," I said.

"Maybe you can make another one," said Grandma.

"I haven't got any foil left," I said.

"Maybe Carla Mae has some," Grandma suggested, "You can go over and ask her."

"She won't have to do that," said Dad quietly. "Just wait a minute." He went through the kitchen and downstairs into the basement, and came back with a dusty box. He handed it to me.

I looked at him for a second and then sat down on his footstool and unwrapped the box. Inside was a wonderful glittery gold star with tiny bells and shiny Christmas balls trimming the front of it.

"It's the niftiest star I ever saw in my whole life!" I said. "Where'd you get it, Dad?"

"It was . . . put away," he said hesitantly .

I saw Grandma smile and go back into the kitchen then, as though she wanted to leave us alone.

"I . . . I was saving it," he said.

"For what?"

"Well, for our tree, I guess."

"It shines! Gee, Dad, it must've cost a lot of money!"

"Your mother made it," he said quietly, and he sat down in his chair beside me.

"My mother made this? She must've been an artist!"

"She . . . liked to paint and draw, the way you do."

"I didn't know that! Nobody ever told me that!"

"She made this star for your first Christmas tree."

"I don't remember . . . I don't remember."

"You were only a few months old. She made presents for you, too."

"What?"

"Knitted booties and a sweater. And she made you a bib with a . . . a big yellow duck in the middle of it."

"A bib? Was I a messy eater then too?" I asked, laughing. "Didn't my mother give me any toys?"

"There was a thing—it was like a bunch of jingle bells suspended from a ribbon. We tied it across your crib, and when you kicked at it, the bells rang. . . ."

"Wow. Do you think I look like my mother? Grandma says I do!"

He gave me a look that seemed a little sad, and then smiled. "You've got the same hair . . . you look like her, especially when you smile."

"Did I smile a lot when I was a baby?"

"Yeah, but your mother said it was indigestion. She'd put you on her shoulder and rub your back . . ."

"Oh, I wish I could remember! What else did my mother do?"

"Well, she sang to you . . ."

"Is my voice like hers? When I sing?"

"The other night, during that Christmas carol . . . you sounded like her."

"I'm a real combination, aren't I? Because I'm going to be very tall, like you!"

He smiled at me, and I held out the star to him.

"Put it on the tree, Dad."

Instead of taking the star from me, he picked me up in his arms and held me up high so I could put the star on the tree. I placed it carefully on the top branch, and he put me down.

"It looks terrific, Dad!"

"It's yours now, Addie," he said, and I turned and put my arms around him, and he hugged me close.

# Epilogue

WE NEVER TALKED to each other about what happened to us that Christmas—we still weren't much for telling our feelings in my family—and I won't pretend that it solved everything between my father and me. We continued to do enthusiastic battle for another twenty years. But after that, each of us knew that there was a person somewhere behind the defenses on the other side, and we never forgot it.

We had a Christmas tree every year after that. Even after my grandmother had died and I had moved away to the city, and my father was there all alone, he would have a tree waiting in the living room when I came home for Christmas, and we would decorate it together. And when it was all finished, I would unwrap the star and put it on the top. Then we would both stand back and admire it and not say much, but I know we were both thinking of that Christmas in 1946.